"It's the city Daddy lived in when he was little."
"Wow! Philadelphia must be OLD!"

"One is all you can take. That's final."

FAMILY CIRCUS®

WE DIDN'T DO IT!

Bil Keane

FAWCETT GOLD MEDAL • NEW YORK

A Fawcett Gold Medal Book
Published by Ballantine Books
Copyright © 1984, 1985 by Cowles Syndicate
Copyright © 1989 by King Features Syndicate, Inc.

Library of Congress Catalog Card Number: 88-92198

ISBN 0-449-13378-8

Manufactured in the United States of America

First Edition: April 1989

"If I lived here I'd NEVER learn to spell my address."

"Is that REALLY William Penn up there or is it just a little William Penn doll?"

"Betsy Ross sewed the first flag."
"Why? Was it torn?"

"Wish WE lived here in Elfreth's Alley. Mommy
would let us play in the street."

"Are all the restaurants in Philadelphia this little?"

"Oh, boy! We're gonna see Inny-pennance Hall
and Delivery Bell!"

"Know what cracked it? They rang it too hard
when Rocky won his fight."

"Mommy! Look! In the City of Brotherly Love!"

"Didn't our forefathers have any famous old amusements we could go on?"

"Scrabble? We're gonna play a word game
before breakfast?"

"Jeffy! Come back here with my pretzel!
Oooh! I hate you, Jeffy!"

"Is mint the only flavor they have?"

"We studied 'bout Benjamin Franklin in school.
He discovered the kite!"

"Go ahead and touch it, PJ...it's all right,
honey....You can pick it up, Jeffy...you're
allowed! Go on, touch something...."

"Let's go, Rocky! You've posed there
long enough."

"If it was snowin' hard when Washington's army got off the turnpike, why didn't they just stay at a motel?"

"Benjamin Franklin was a great statesman,
a scientist, an inventor, an author...."

"Besides the soft pretzels my favorite part of the
trip was when the Phillies won in the ninth!"

"Barfy keeps putting tourniquets on trees."

"Look, Mommy! Some little green whiskers!"

"We're building a beach!"

"Aw, Mommy! You let Daddy get a buzz haircut
when he was little!"

"I've never been airsick, but I've been
groundsick a lot."

"Daddy took us window-fishing!"

"It's an Australian Frisbee!"

"I 'member seein' that torch before. The
Statue of Liberty was holdin' it."

"He isn't break dancing. He's scratchin' his back."

"PJ's practicin' the long jump. He's up
to one foot."

"I'm passing the torch to you."

"On your market, get set...."

"Are you helping him think?"

"Did you see that jump? Too bad there isn't
an Olympics for cats."

"Betcha I could win a gold medal if they
had hopscotch."

"It's Billy's soap-on-a-rope. We're
playing Olympics."

"OK, Mommy! Now you get a turn to take
us all in!"

"Is there any hope of a teachers' strike
this year, Mommy?"

"Miss McElfresh got left back. She's still
in the same room as last year."

"Barfy! You have 'trocious floor manners!"

"Give me back my good white glove, Michael Jackson, or I'm tellin' Mommy!"

"I'm sorry, but you're not using my
leg-warmers as shinguards."

"The coffee table is NOT for break-dancing!"

"I'm flossing my comb's teeth."

"But, Mommy! What about all the dirt
I track OUT?"

"I'm comin' in 'cause if lightning hit me it
would mess up my hair."

"Is it Daddy?" "No...." "Billy?" "No...."
"Barfy?" "No...."

"Did I hear somebody spooning ice cream?"

"We're goin' to an operetta tonight—'The Pirates of Pennzoil.'"

"Try not to fall down, P.J.
You're clumsy, you know."

"They gave it a PG-13 rating, but it seemed
more like a PG-21 to me."

"Hi, Grandma! Wanna hear my
Tarzan yell?"

"I wasn't the last one in. Barfy was!"

"I can't crayon when you're drivin'."

"I don't suppose you know what happened to the batteries out of my radio."

"Daddy says I ask a lot of questions. Do you
think I ask a lot of questions?"

"Fee-fi-fo-fum! I smell the blood of
an English muffin!"

"That was the pencil sharpener for heaven's
sake, not the can opener."

"PJ littered! He threw his shoe out
the window!"

"That was gonna be our clubhouse, but we
ran out of summer."

"Mary had a little lamp, little lamp...."

"Well, basically, I keep saying 'basically'
'cause everybody else does. I guess
that's the only reason, basically."

"Could we have just one more piece, please, Mommy? We'll eat every bit of our dinner, WE PROMISE!"

"Hi, Doctor Shackelford." "That's our, dentist!"

"Mrs. Miles' new baby sure has pink teeth."

"Will there be less homework if the
Democrats win the election?"

"Here comes its motor now."

"I'm glad they don't keep stopping
the clock like that in school."

"Mommy, did you know that Christopher
Columbus invented America?"

"This was in the basement with no picture
in it, but don't worry — I'll draw one!"

"We just figured it out, Mommy. When I'm 19, all four of us will be teen-agers at the same time!"

"First the good news: I scored a touchdown."

"We're in the closet watchin' Kittycat's
eyes glow in the dark."

"He's too big to block, so try
ticklin' him."

"It has turtle wrists, too."

"Go to your room, young lady."

"This caterpillar isn't walkin'. He's
wrinklin' along."

"Wanna hold my caterpillar awhile, Grandma?
It's OK — he's dead."

"Here's my report card. I'm on the A-Team
in two subjects."

"I am not looking for a movie to take you
children to. I'm trying to find one I
can take grandma to."

"Mommy, would you make my hair in knots like Julie's?"

"It's just the storm before the lull."

"Mommy, my voice hurts."

"What homework is that?"
"Handwriting."

"Some of these notes are jumping
over the fence."

"Why do you always make the edge of
the pie look like corduroy?"

"Hold up your hands, Jeffy. I need
more fingers to count on."

"Know who Jack-O'-Lantern's wife is?
Jackie O."

"Daddy guessed me!"

"Sorry, Barfy. Nobody gave out any
doggy treats."

"If it's a sport jacket why won't you
let me play football in it?"

"How much did you get, Daddy?"

"Call the Ghostbusters!"

"I get an A in art if I hang this poster where everyone in the house can see it!"

"Lost your mittens? You naughty
kitten! Then you shall have
no pie."

"All the puddles are crunchy!"

"If I have a cold why am I so HOT?"

"It's easy to quit smokin' cigarettes. You just take it out of your mouth!"

"I won't tell the children
we're coming, Mom —
'til we're all packed."

"When do we leave for
Grandma's?"

"They have doggy bags in case we
don't finish our dinner."

"Some clouds got in my ears, but I yawned
and they popped out."

"Daddy, get one with a stick shift, and bucket seats, and sunroof, and tape deck, and. . . ."

"Maybe granddad and grandma forgot we were comin' and went out."

"I think he was expectin' you to be
our OTHER grandma."

"Grandma really likes all the drawings we
sent her. They're hangin' everywhere!"

"Mommy always takes the crust off
our baloney."

"Grandma got out some of mommy's toys
from when she was little, but we're
only allowed to look at them."

"I'm tired, Granddad! Carry me?"

"Grandma said she was gonna DRESS the turkey. Did she forget?"

"The trees around here are really OLD,
Granddad. Bet some of 'em are over
30 or even 40."

"It's a good thing you had your stairway
padded, Grandma!"

"Mum! Are you dredging up my childhood
escapades again?"

"Granddad, what were you when you were
old enough to work?"

"I like our paper at home better. I know where to find the comics."

"Granddad sure takes us a lot of wheres."

"When we have childrens, Grandma and Granddad will become great."

"Grandma isn't crying. She just got somethin'
in her eye. It happened the day we
came, too."

"There's one thing from their visit they left behind that we'll NEVER send back—memories!"

"Thank you, Daddy! You found
my mitten!"

"You won't hafta BUY stamps any more,
Mommy. I'll DRAW them for you!"

"Who left the TV set turned off?"

"These 'lectric scissors make my
hand dizzy."

"Didn't you hear Daddy? No running through the house."

"Of all living creatures
humans are the only
ones who pray."

"Or
need
to."